Silly Chicken

BY

Rukhsana Khan

PICTURES BY

Yunmee Kyong

VIKING

VIKING
Published by Penguin Group
Penguin Young Readers Group, 345 Hudson Street, New York, New York 10014, U.S.A.

Penguin Books Ltd, Registered Offices: 80 Strand, London WC2R 0RL, England

First published in 2005 by Viking, a division of Penguin Young Readers Group

1   3   5   7   9   10   8   6   4   2

LIBRARY OF CONGRESS CATALOGING-IN-PUBLICATION DATA
Khan, Rukhsana, date-
Silly chicken / by Rukhsana Khan ; illustrated by Yunmee Kyong.
p. cm.
Summary: In Pakistan, Rani believes that her mother loves their pet chicken Bibi more than
she cares for her, until the day that a fluffy chick appears and steals Rani's own affections.
ISBN 0-670-05912-9 (hardcover)
[1. Jealousy—Fiction 2. Chickens—Fiction. 3. Mother and child—Fiction. 4. Pets—Fiction. 5. Pakistan—Fiction.]
I. Kyong, Yunmee, ill. II. Title.
PZ7.K52654Si 2005   [E]—dc22   2004015830

Set in Goudy Newstyle
Manufactured in China

To Nusaybah, my silly buchi —R.K.

For my parents —Y.K.

Ami loves her hen better than me.
She calls her Bibi. I call her Silly.
     She's always fussing over whether
I fed Bibi. Did I give her clean water?
     I want to ask, "What's the point?
She'll only make it dirty."

She's such a silly hen. I've never seen a chicken like her. She's taller than any other chicken, with long, gangly legs and a silly look on her face.

She acts more like an old woman than a chicken. She follows Ami around the yard wherever she goes. Even into the house!

Chickens belong in the yard.

Somehow that silly hen has wormed her way in. It started when she got sick. Have you ever heard a chicken sneeze? They sound so funny!

"Aw hai! Poor thing!" said Ami. "She's got a cold! No wonder she won't lay any eggs."

At first Ami nursed her outside, but when night came, she brought her in. "Let's make a nest for her in the cupboard," she said, and made me fetch sticks from the yard. I had to pile them together, and she took my dress to put on top for that hen to sit on.

"But Ami! That's my dress!"

"It's a rag now. Let her have it."

"No! I still want it!"

"Don't be silly."

When I turned to go to my room, I bumped my leg and started crying. Ami hardly even looked at it. Told me I'd be fine.

I wish she'd never got that silly hen. What good is a hen that won't lay eggs? Dinner!

A few days later, an amazing thing happened. Bibi laid an egg. She was walking around the yard and let out the strangest *squaaaawk!* The egg fell right where she was standing. It landed with a crack.

Silly hen. Didn't even know she's supposed to sit to lay an egg.

Ami showed her. Brought her to the nest and explained how it was done. Bibi cocked her head and listened. When Ami was done talking, Bibi sat down on the nest just as if she'd understood. Show-off!

Ami was so proud. "Look how smart she is!"
Ami never said I was smart.

When Ami's back was turned, I whispered, "I'd like to cook you
up and eat you!"

Bibi just watched me with a silly look on her face. She hadn't
understood anything at all.

When Bibi laid another egg (in the nest), Ami showed all the neighbors the "fine egg" as if it was a miracle.

Then she told me to put the egg in a tiny dish and set it in a cupboard. We'd have it later.

One day, Ami took me to visit my father's grave. We went by tonga. I just love the clip-clop of the horse's hooves. I wasn't scared, because Ami was there and it was daytime.

When we got back, Ami couldn't find Bibi anywhere.

We checked the yard. We checked in every cupboard. We checked up and down the road and asked the neighbors.

Then we saw the dog prints in the dirt and a few of Bibi's feathers. The gate had been shut. I was sure I shut it. I even locked it. But Ami still blamed me.

I felt bad.

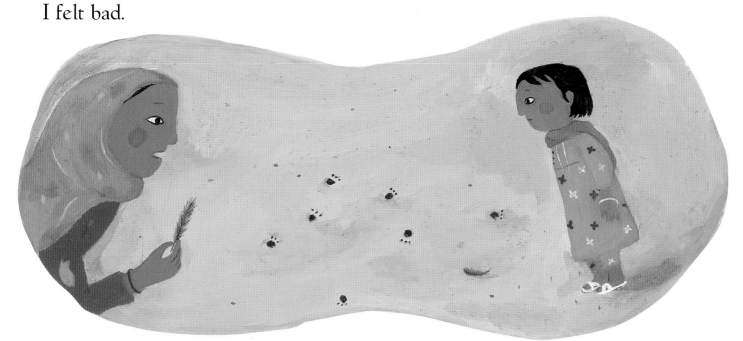

The next few days were very hot and humid. Even for Pakistan.
Ami mostly stayed inside. I brought her tall glasses of ice cold lussi. I
fanned her and fussed over her, but it didn't do much good.
    She missed Bibi.

About two weeks later, she was finally up and around. She was
mopping the floor when she said, "Rani, I hear something."
"What, Ami?"
"Sssssh. It will come again."

We were both silent for the longest while. Just as I was about to say something, I heard it, too.

Ami's eyes were huge. "What is it? A burglar, you think?"

We waited an awfully long time. Then we heard it again. It was in the kitchen.

Ami followed a few steps behind me.

Every time the sound came I moved closer, till finally I came to one of the cupboards in the kitchen.

"It's in there," I said.

"Open it," whispered Ami.

"What if it's a rat?"

"Come now. Open it. That's a good girl. I'm right behind you."

So I did.

I saw the little bowl and took it down. In it was the cutest, fluffiest little chick I'd ever seen and a couple of eggshells.

I named her Bibi Ki Buchi. It means Bibi's child. But we call her Buchi for short.

Ami says I love Buchi even more than I love her, but that's just silly.

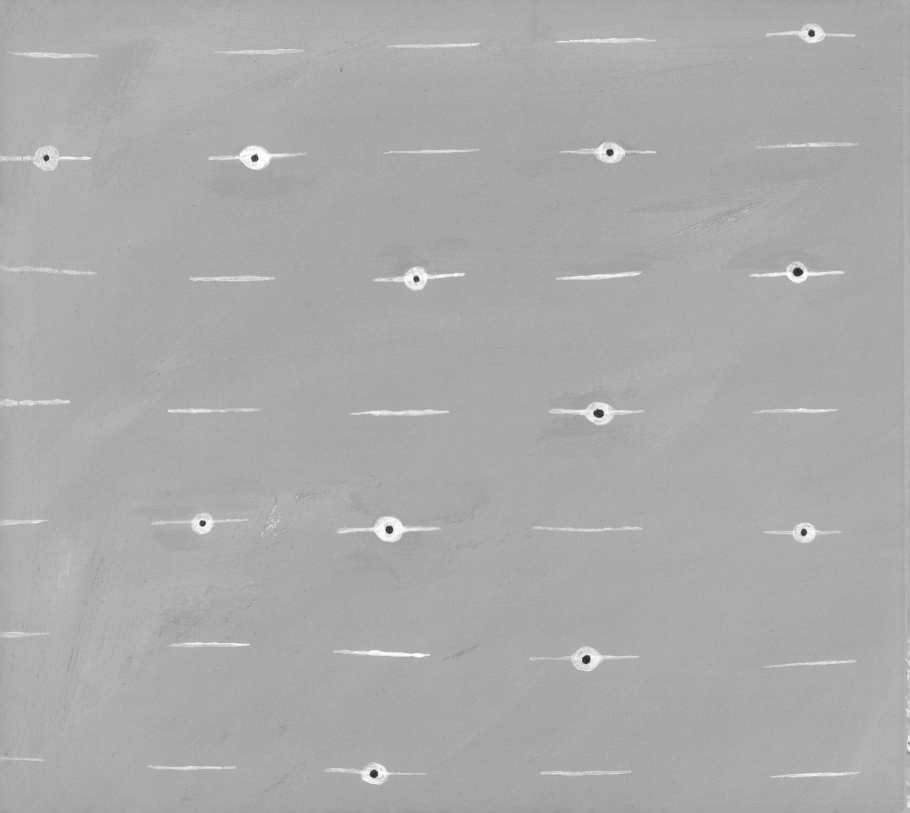